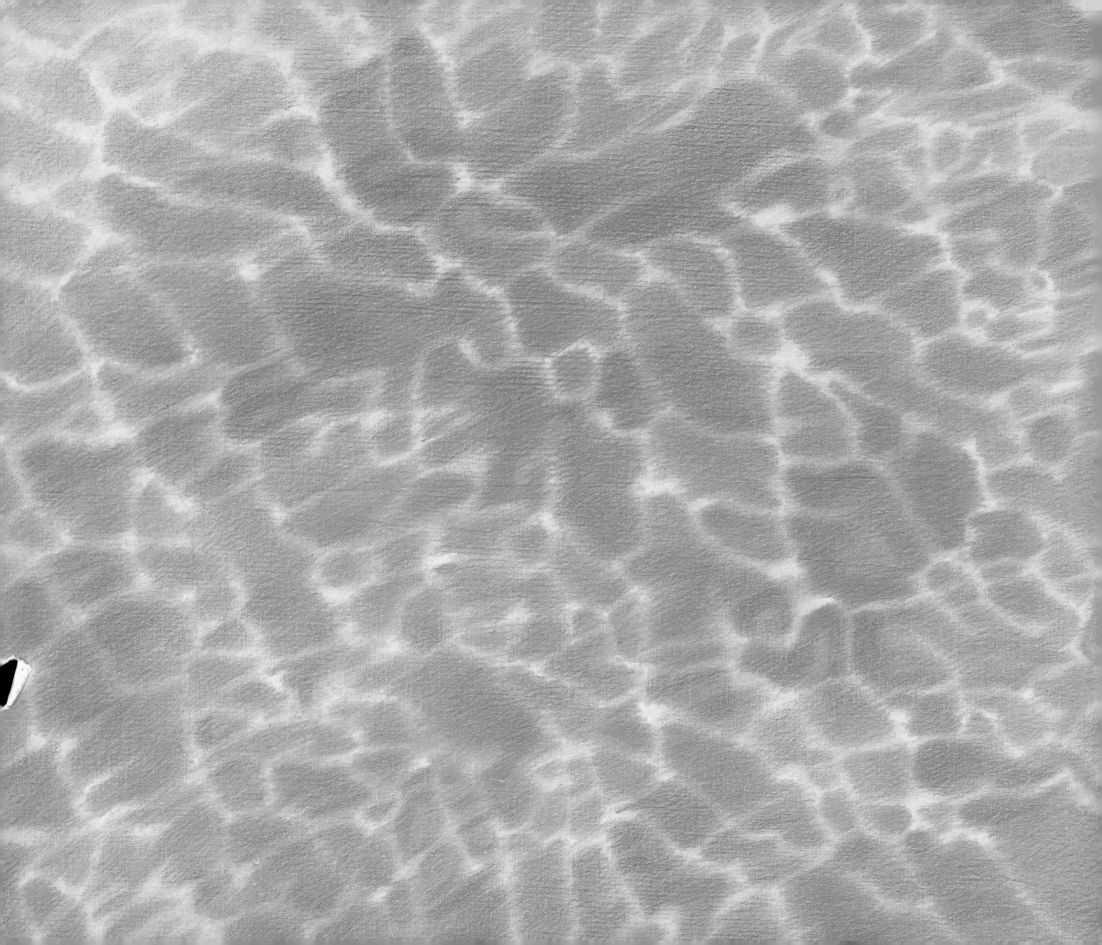

for Lenny - R. A.

for Anne & Iain Campbell - I. A.

A TEMPLAR BOOK

First published in the UK in 2007 by Templar Publishing.
This softback edition published in 2008 by Templar Publishing,
an imprint of The Templar Company plc,
The Granary, North Street, Dorking, Surrey, RH4 1DN, UK
www.templarco.co.uk

First softback edition

ISBN 978-1-84011-856-8

Designed by Mike Jolley
Edited by Sue Harris

Printed in China

templar publishing

WATER BOY

Ros Asquith * illustrated by Ian Andrew

Water boy, water boy, what do you see?

I see big waves in the foaming sea.

I see seagulls circling high,

Boats and starfish and a stormy sky.

I laugh at the dog as he races to play,
and paddles in puddles and shakes off the spray.

Sand boy, sand boy, what do you do?

I pour the sand into my shoe.

I pour it in, I run about, I swing my shoe, the sand flies out!

I laugh at the dog running into the sea.

I knock down my sandcastle – clever old me!

Mud boy, mud boy, where do you play?
   I play in the mud the live-long day.
   I splash it and throw it around everywhere.
   I get mud on my clothes, on my face, in my hair.

I laugh at the dog, muddy as me.
We're just as muddy as we can be.

Grass boy, grass boy, what do you smell?
I smell cowslips and nodding bluebells.
I smell the fresh grass, I smell a red rose,
I smell manure, I wrinkle my nose.

Farm boy, farm boy, what do you hear?
    I hear cows moo, hens clucking near.
    I hear the harvester making hay,
    I hear sheep bleat and horses neigh.

I laugh at the dog, he's seen the farm cat.
He's trying to catch her —
she won't like that.

Bath boy, bath boy, what do you do?
  I splash the bubbles all over you!
  I squeeze slippy soap, I laugh like a drain,
  I splash the water again and again.

I laugh at the dog attacking the mat.
He pretends the mat is the old farm cat.

Bed boy, bed boy, what do you love?

My pillow below, my blanket above.

My mum with a story, my cuddly ted,

My dreams of adventure, my cosy bed.

I love my dog, curled up so tight,
I love... y... a... a... awn, night, night...

... we'll dream of tomorrow 'til morning light.

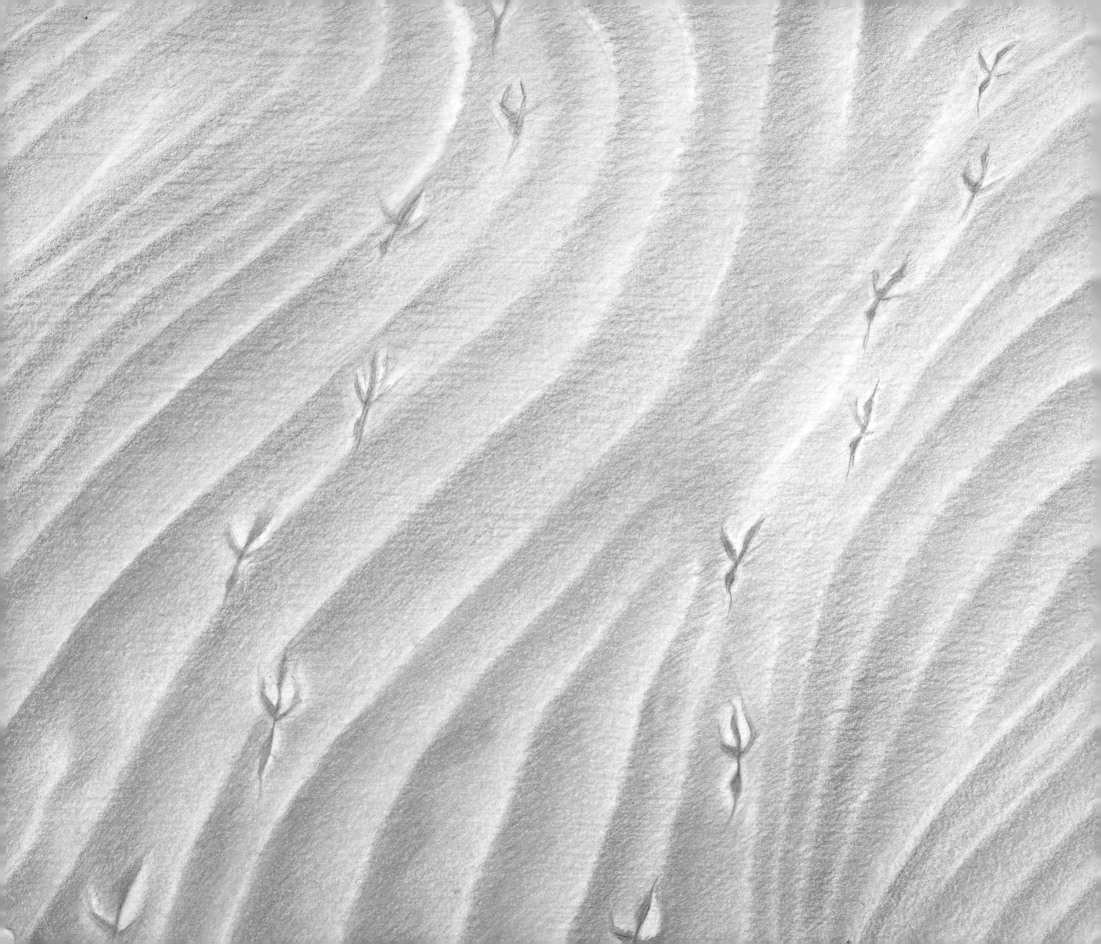